Crazy about puppies?

Ready for crime-busting?

Want to know about real life police dogs?

'GILL LEWIS, a former vet, is a major talent'
– THE TIMES

SCOUT

May c...
saus...

Welcome to Sausage Dreams **Puppy Academy**, where a team of plucky young pups are learning how to be all sorts of working dogs. Let's meet some of the students...

Scout
the SMART ONE!

BREED German shepherd
SPECIAL SKILL
Sniffing out crime

STAR
the speedy one!

BREED Border collie

SPECIAL SKILL
Sensing danger

PiP
the friendly one!

BREED Labrador

SPECIAL SKILL
Ball games

MURPHY
the big one!

BREED Leonberger

SPECIAL SKILL
Swimming

...and some of the teachers:

MAJOR BONES

One of the teachers at the
Sausage Dreams **Puppy Academy**.
Known for being strict.

PROFESSOR OFFENBACH

Head of the Sausage Dreams **Puppy Academy**. She is a small dog with A VERY LOUD VOICE!

OXFORD
UNIVERSITY PRESS

Great Clarendon Street, Oxford OX2 6DP
Oxford University Press is a department of the University of Oxford.
It furthers the University's objective of excellence in research, scholarship,
and education by publishing worldwide in

Oxford   New York

Auckland   Cape Town   Dar es Salaam   Hong Kong   Karachi
Kuala Lumpur   Madrid   Melbourne   Mexico City   Nairobi
New Delhi   Shanghai   Taipei   Toronto

With offices in

Argentina   Austria   Brazil   Chile   Czech Republic   France   Greece
Guatemala   Hungary   Italy   Japan   Poland   Portugal   Singapore
South Korea   Switzerland   Thailand   Turkey   Ukraine   Vietnam

Oxford is a registered trade mark of Oxford University Press
in the UK and in certain other countries

British Library Cataloguing in Publication Data

Data available

ISBN: 978-0-19-273920-9

1 3 5 7 9 10 8 6 4 2

Printed and bound by CPI Group (UK) Ltd, Croydon, CR0 4YY

Paper used in the production of this book is a natural,
recyclable product made from wood grown in sustainable forests
The manufacturing process conforms to the environmental
regulations of the country of origin

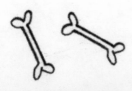

GILL LEWIS

PUPPY ACADEMY

Scout
AND THE SAUSAGE THIEF

OXFORD
UNIVERSITY PRESS

1

Scout hid behind the stack of
baked-bean cans and waited. The
supermarket was busy with Saturday
morning shoppers. She knew this
was the moment when Frank Furter,
the notorious sausage thief, would
strike again. He could steal a salami
from a sandwich or a hot dog from
a hot-dog stand without ever being
seen. No police dog had caught him
in action yet.

No one knew just how Frank Furter stole the sausages. But Scout thought she knew. She'd worked it out and now she was ready. She looked up at the ceiling of the supermarket and waited for Frank's next move.

High above people's heads, one white ceiling tile slid slowly sideways. Frank's face appeared in the gap, spying down on the fresh meat counter. Scout could see the bungee rope tied around his chest. She'd have to be quick on her feet to catch him.

Down came Frank.

'Gotcha!' shouted Scout.

She pounced, wrapping the string of sausages round and round him, tying him up in a big sausage knot.

Everyone cheered. Frank Furter had been caught at last and Scout was their hero.

'Scout!'

'Scout!'

Scout woke up from her daydream.

'Come on, Scout,' said her mum. 'Finish your breakfast. You can't be late for school today.'

'Do you think Frank Furter will ever be caught?' said Scout.

Scout's dad put down his paper. 'He's very clever. No one has worked out just how he steals the sausages.'

'But how do you know it's him?' asked Scout.

'Frank's pawprints are found all over the crime scenes,' said Scout's dad. He shook his head. 'Your mum and I have been working on this investigation for months. If we don't catch him before the weekend, the village sausage festival will have to be cancelled.'

'Cancelled?' said Scout. 'But it's

the most famous sausage festival in the world.'

'I know,' said Mum. 'But unless Frank is caught, no one's sausages are safe. These are dark times. There hasn't been a case like this since Peppa Roni the Italian Spinoni hijacked Burt the Butcher's lorry.'

Scout frowned. 'If anyone can catch Frank, you and Dad can.'

Scout's mum sighed. 'I hope so, Scout. I hope so.'

Scout's mum and dad were well-known police dogs. They were loved by the villagers and feared by burglars. Until the recent spate of sausage robberies, there hadn't been a crime in Little Barking for three years.

'Frank trained to be a police dog with us when we were at Puppy Academy,' said Scout's mum. 'He had a thing about sausages even back then.'

'Frank Furter was a police dog!' said Scout. 'But he should know not to break the law.'

Scout's dad looked across at her. 'There have been a few police dogs who have forgotten their vows.'

Scout put her paw to her chest. 'I vow to be honest, brave, and true, and to serve my fellow dogs and humans too.'

'And above all else, be kind,' smiled Scout's mum. 'I'm sure you will make a great police dog one day.'

Scout puffed out her chest in pride. She was a German shepherd.

She wanted to be a police dog like her mum and dad one day too. She wanted to catch burglars, find lost children, and keep people in Little Barking safe.

'You look smart in your new collar,' said Scout's dad.

'I have to look my best today,' said Scout. 'Our first test for our Care in the Community badge is to present ourselves smartly to Major Bones.'

Scout went to the Sausage Dreams Puppy Academy for working dogs, where she was training to become a police dog. There were all sorts of puppies at the academy. Some were training to be sheepdogs, others were training for water rescue or mountain rescue, and others to assist humans who were blind or

hard of hearing. There were so many
different jobs for the puppies to
choose from.

'Don't forget your coat,' said
Scout's mum. 'There's more rain
forecast for today.'

Scout's dad looked out at the water pooling outside the kennel. 'The river is rising and the duck brigade is on standby for any flooding. The new houses by the river are at risk if it keeps on raining like this.'

Scout put on her coat and looked at the row of badges she'd earned so far. She hoped she could add the Care in the Community badge by the end of the day.

Scout set off for the Puppy Academy. Despite the rain, she was feeling happy. She trotted through the high street of Little Barking. The village was busy with humans on their way to work and to school. Ahead, a crowd had gathered outside the butcher's shop. Scout pushed her way through to find out what the fuss was about.

Burt the Butcher was standing in the doorway, red-faced and shaking his fist in the air. The meat trays

in his shop window were sausage-less.

'The sausage thief has struck
again!' shouted Burt.

There were gasps of horror from
the crowd.

'The sausage festival will be cancelled,' wailed one woman.

Scout looked around at the shocked faces, but she knew it was too late to do anything. Frank Furter, the master cold-meats criminal, would be far away already.

Scout set off again. She was weaving her way in and out of parents with pushchairs and children on their way to school when she stumbled on something on the ground.

It was a threadbare teddy with a missing eye, and a sticking plaster on its paw. It lay in a puddle with a big muddy footprint on its tummy.

It looked sad and lonely. Scout sniffed
it. Beneath the mud and water, it
smelled of strawberry shampoo and
cheese and pickle sandwiches.

Scout knew that someone loved
this teddy. She looked around to see
if she could see anyone looking for it,
but everyone was hurrying to get out
of the rain.

A human child must have
dropped this on the way to school,
she thought. Maybe she should take
it to the school, but she knew that
would make her late for her test.
Maybe she should leave it here.
Whoever lost it might find it on the
way home.

Scout sat the teddy on a bench
and walked on, but deep inside she
just knew that someone wanted this
teddy back. She couldn't leave it.
Scout turned around, picked up the
teddy, and trotted to the school. She
followed the long line of children
to the school gates. A small girl

smelling of strawberry shampoo was
sobbing in her mother's arms.

Scout trotted up and pushed the
teddy into the girl's hands.

'Eddie!' cried the girl, 'you're
alive!' She hugged her teddy tight
against her.

'Clever pup,' said the girl's mother, patting Scout on the head. 'How ever did you find him?'

Scout wanted to tell her where she'd found the teddy, but she knew humans didn't understand woofs and barks, so she just wagged her tail instead.

The girl reached into her bag and offered Scout a cheese and pickle sandwich, but at that moment the school bell rang and Scout knew it was time for her to go to school too.

She turned and ran. She couldn't be late. She had to make it to Puppy Academy in time.

2

Scout ran out of the school. If she took the shortcut through the park she might be able to get to the academy in time for the first test. She squeezed through the hedge, the brambles catching and sticking in her fur. Her feet raced across the field, the mud flying up from her paws.

As she ran through the academy

gates she could see her class lining up in the hall. She rushed in to join them, mud and rain dripping from her coat, brambles stuck in her fur and collar.

'Where have you been?' whispered Lulu.

'We've been waiting for you,' said Murphy.

'You're late!' Major Bones glared at her. Major Bones was one of the teachers at Puppy Academy and he was known for being strict.

'I'm sorry,' panted Scout, 'but . . . '

'No buts,' woofed Major Bones. He looked Scout up and down. 'You look like you've been dragged through a hedge!'

'I have . . . ' began Scout.

Major Bones tutted. 'You do realize smart presentation is one of your Care in the Community tests today?'

'Yes,' said Scout. 'I . . . '

'No excuses, Scout. I can't pass

you looking like that. Now go and get yourself cleaned up and join us for the zebra crossing test.'

Scout ran off, her tail between her legs. She tried to brush the mud from her fur, but it stuck in thick clumps and she couldn't remove it all. It would have to do.

She rejoined Major Bones and the other pups in the hall. Rain hammered on the roof above.

'Normally, we would do the zebra crossing test outside,' said Major Bones, 'but, as it's raining, we'll take the test in the hall today.'

The pups all looked at the zebra crossing chalked on the ground. Scout felt her legs shaking. She hadn't had a good start. She had to do well in this next test, she had to.

'We're very lucky to have Mrs Chubbs, the pet shop owner, here today,' woofed Major Bones. 'She has volunteered to be our human in need, and she has generously donated a large bag of Crunchie Munchies for you all to share after the test.'

All the puppies barked and wagged their tails. Crunchie Munchies were everyone's favourite treats.

'Today I will be testing you on how to help someone across a busy road,' woofed Major Bones.

Mrs Chubbs shuffled onto the training ground. She walked slowly with the help of a stick. She gave all the puppies a little wave. Scout sat up straight, her feet together and her

ears pricked up. She wanted Major
Bones to know she could do this.

'Let's have Murphy first,' said
Major Bones.

Murphy trotted forward. He
took Mrs Chubbs gently by the
sleeve, looked left and right and left
again, and guided
her over the
crossing.

'Well done, well done,' said Major Bones. 'I hope everyone was watching Murphy, because that's how to do it.'

Murphy trotted back to the line of puppies, his head held high.

'Now, let's have Scout,' woofed
Major Bones.

Scout felt nervous. She didn't
want to mess this up. Her muscles
were in tight knots.

She grabbed Mrs Chubbs.

'Ow!! Oooh! My arm!' cried Mrs
Chubbs.

Scout let go. In her rush, she'd
grabbed Mrs Chubbs's arm, not her
sleeve. Scout backed away, knocking
Mrs Chubbs's walking stick from
under her.

'SCOUT! BE CAREFUL!'
bellowed Major Bones, as Mrs
Chubbs clattered to the ground.

Scout looked between Mrs
Chubbs and Major Bones. 'I didn't
mean to! I'm sorry.'

Major Bones helped Mrs Chubbs
to her feet. He shook his head. 'I
don't know what's got into you
today, Scout. I think you'd better
come and see me in my office. I
don't think you're up to taking the
rest of your Care in the Community
tests today.'

3

Scout stood and waited for Major Bones in his office. There were piles of papers everywhere, boxes stuffed with books, and drawers bursting with pens and pencils. There were agility hoops and jumps packed against the back wall. Scout couldn't even see the surface of the desk.

'Ah, Scout,' said Major Bones, coming into the room. 'Sit down, sit down.'

Scout looked around but couldn't see a spare seat beneath the mess.

Major Bones sat down in his chair. 'So, Scout. I'm here to listen. In your own words, tell me what went wrong today.'

'Well . . .' said Scout. 'I . . .'

RING! RING! RING! RING!

'Excuse me,' said Major Bones,

'I'd better take that call.'

Major Bones searched under boxes and piles of paper.

'Now, where did I put that phone?' he muttered.

He searched and searched until the phone rang off.

'Never mind,' said Major Bones.

RINGGGG.

'Where were we . . . ah, yes! Well, Scout. I'm sorry to say that I won't be able to award you the Care in the Community badge today. You haven't passed the presentation test or the zebra crossing test.' He frowned. 'Really, Scout, I'm not sure you even want this badge. Take a good look at yourself. You've come to school plastered in mud and brambles.'

Scout stared down at the floor. She hadn't had a chance to tell her side of the story. 'I'm sorry,' she whimpered.

'Don't worry, young pup,' sighed

Major Bones. 'No harm done. Mrs
Chubbs is fine after her fall. You'll
just have to try a little harder next
time.' He glanced at the mud and
brambles in her coat. 'Maybe avoid
the park next time too.'

Scout nodded, but she had

wanted to pass the test with her friends. She didn't want her mum and dad to know she'd failed.

'In the meantime,' said Major Bones, 'I'd like you to take the bag of Crunchie Munchies to the food shed. The lock has broken, so I'll put you on guard duty until the others have finished their tests.'

Scout helped Major Bones carry the bag across the yard. The rain had stopped, but the clouds looked dark and swollen with more rain. Major Bones placed the Crunchie Munchies in the food shed and closed the door.

'Right, Scout,' he said. 'Your job is to guard the Crunchie Munchies. Can you do that for me?'

Scout nodded. She watched Major Bones walk away to join the other pups in the class and continue the tests without her.

Scout shivered. A cold wind was blowing, finding its way through her thick fur to her skin. She wanted to find shelter but she had to guard the food shed.

While she waited, Scout looked
out across the academy. At the
bottom of the hill she could see
the new housing estate where the
river-meadows used to be. The river
looked brown and swollen and had
risen up to the tops of the banks.

'Hey, Scout! It's break time. Are you OK?'

Scout looked up to see Gwen, Murphy, Scruff, and Lulu walking over to her.

'I'm OK,' she said, trying to sound cheerful. 'How are the tests?'

'They're all right,' said Gwen. 'We had to find a lost child and then rescue a cat from a tree.'

Scout put her head on her paws. She wished she could have done the tests with them too. She was missing all the fun.

'Come and play with us,' woofed Gwen. 'We've got a break until lunchtime.'

Scout shook her head. 'I have to guard the food store.'

'It's not as if anyone's going to steal the treats,' Gwen said.

'You never know,' said Scruff. 'Frank Furter hasn't been caught yet.'

'But he goes after sausages, not Crunchie Munchies,' said Lulu.

'How do you think he steals the sausages?' said Murphy.

'Invisibility cape,' said Gwen. 'That's what my brother says.'

'My dad thinks he's invented a sausage magnet,' woofed Scruff.

'No one knows,' said Scout. 'That's the thing. No one knows how he does it.'

'So you're not coming to play?' said Gwen.

Scout shook her head. Her duty was to guard the food store. Even if she couldn't be a police dog, she could act like one.

'See you later then,' said Murphy.

Scout stayed by the food store. She didn't move. Her stomach rumbled all through lunchtime and into the afternoon. She watched her classmates do the rest of their Care in the Community tests. She watched them picking up litter

and practising to keep the peace
at the sausage festival. Last year
the festival had turned ugly when
Verity's Vegan Sausages scooped first
prize over Burt's Black Pudding.

Scout heard Professor Offenbach
call everyone together in the hall.
Professor Offenbach was the head
of the Sausage Dreams Puppy
Academy. She was a small dog with
a big voice that boomed out across
the academy.

Scout sat and waited by the food
store and listened.

**'WELCOME, PUPS, TO OUR
FRIDAY AWARD CEREMONY. IT'S**

BEEN ANOTHER BUSY WEEK AT THE ACADEMY. TODAY WE HAVE BADGES TO GIVE OUT FOR CARE IN THE COMMUNITY. THIS IS A VERY SPECIAL BADGE INDEED. I'D LIKE TO CALL MURPHY, GWEN, LULU, AND SCRUFF UP ONTO THE GIANT SAUSAGE PODIUM TO RECEIVE THEIR AWARDS.'

Scout wished she could be up on the podium too. What would her mum and dad say when they found out she was the only pup in her class not to receive the badge?

'**AND,**' woofed Professor

Offenbach, **'WE CAN NOW CELEBRATE WITH MRS CHUBBS'S CRUNCHIE MUNCHIES!'**

All the pups cheered, and Scout watched them racing towards her and the food shed. She wasn't sure she felt like Crunchie Munchies any more.

'Hi, Scout,' said Gwen.

'Well done for getting

your Care in the Community badge,'
said Scout. She tried her best to
smile.

'Now then,' said Major Bones.
'Who would like a Crunchie
Munchie?'

The other pups all put their paws
in the air.

Major Bones opened the food
shed and went inside.

He didn't come out with the
Crunchie Munchies. He came out
with a frown on his face instead.
'Scout,' he said, 'have you been here
all this time?'

'I haven't moved a muscle, sir,'

said Scout.

'Has anyone been in the food shed?'

'No,' said Scout.

Major Bones walked all the way around the food shed and bent down to look Scout in the eye. 'Are you sure?'

'Yes,' said Scout. 'No one else has

been here.'

Major Bones looked across them all. 'We have a problem,' he said.

The puppies all looked at each other.

Major Bones pulled himself up to his full height. 'The problem is, the Crunchie Munchies . . . are missing!'

4

'Impossible,' said Scout. 'I haven't seen anyone carry the bag away.'

'It isn't the bag that is missing,' said Major Bones. 'The bag is still there. The Crunchie Munchies have disappeared. Someone has eaten them all.'

The pups all fell silent. Scout could feel their eyes on her.

'How could that happen?' Scout

piped up. 'I was here all the time.'

Lulu frowned. 'No wonder you wanted to stay by the food shed. You wanted to eat the Crunchie Munchies all by yourself.'

'No!' said Scout.

Murphy pointed his paw at her. 'Maybe you were jealous of us so you ate them because you didn't want us to have them too.'

'That's not true!' said Scout. How could they think that about her?

Scruff scrunched her nose up. 'Well, tell us where they are.'

'I . . . I . . . can't,' said Scout, looking at them all. She put her head in the shed to see the empty bag on the floor. 'They've just disappeared.'

'Disappeared in your tummy, you mean,' said Gwen. 'We were looking forward to those treats. We deserved them, not you.'

'Ahem,' said Major Bones. 'Let's not jump to conclusions. Let's think about this logically. So, the Crunchie Munchies were placed in the shed.'

'Correct,' said Scout.

'And you guarded the door,' said Major Bones.

'Correct,' said Scout.

'You saw no one enter or leave the building?'

'No one,' said Scout.

Major Bones walked all the way around the shed. 'There are no other doors or windows to the shed.'

Scout followed him. 'No.'

'Hmm!' said Major Bones. 'You see, Scout, you are the only pup to have been near the Crunchie Munchies. I'm afraid it's beginning to look very suspicious.'

'I didn't eat them,' said Scout. 'Maybe it was Frank Furter. No one has caught him stealing yet.'

Gwen narrowed her eyes. 'But he only steals sausages.'

'Admit it, Scout,' whispered Lulu. 'You're the thief.'

'Thief! Thief! Thief!' Angry puppy faces closed in on Scout.

'NO!' wailed Scout, looking wildly around at them all.

'That's enough,' Major Bones said to the pups. He turned to Scout. 'I'm afraid you must come with me. I will need to see you in my office with Professor Offenbach while we decide just what to do.'

Scout stood in Major Bones's office for the second time that day. She stared at her paws. She felt like a criminal. She even felt guilty though she knew she hadn't done anything wrong.

'Hmmm!' said Major Bones, again. 'This is a difficult situation.'

'VERY DIFFICULT,' boomed Professor Offenbach.

'Scout,' said Major Bones. 'We're
here to listen to your side of the
story. Please tell us, in your own
words, what happened today with
the Crunchie Munchies.'

RING! RING! RING! RING!

'Excuse me,' said Major Bones. 'I
should take that call.'

Major Bones lifted up piles of paper and boxes. 'Now, where did I put that phone?' he muttered.

Professor Offenbach rolled her eyes.

Major Bones searched until the phone rang off.

'Never mind,' he said. 'Now, where were we? Ah, yes. You see, Scout, we're in a very difficult situation. You were put in charge of the Crunchie Munchies and now they have gone missing. I'm afraid the paw of blame seems to be pointing at you.'

Scout stared at them wide-eyed. She couldn't believe what they were suggesting. They hadn't even heard her side of the story.

'OF COURSE, WE'RE NOT BLAMING YOU AT THIS STAGE,' barked Professor Offenbach, **'BUT UNTIL WE FIND OUT EXACTLY**

WHAT HAPPENED, WE WILL HAVE TO ASK YOU TO LEAVE THE ACADEMY.'

'Leave?' said Scout.

'I'm afraid so,' said Major Bones. 'We need to find out what happened to the missing Crunchie Munchies. We don't know who took them, but

we will find out. We can't have liars and thieves within the academy.'

'I didn't do it,' blurted Scout. 'You do believe me, don't you?' She searched both their faces. 'Don't you?'

Major Bones fiddled with some papers on his desk.

Professor Offenbach put a paw on her shoulder and looked down at her with sad eyes.

Scout didn't want to stay a minute longer. She turned away from them both, and ran.

5

Leave the academy? It was an impossible thought. Now she would never be a police dog, ever.

The other pups were waiting for her outside.

'Why did you do it?' Murphy said. 'We would have shared our treats with you.'

'I didn't. Please believe me,' pleaded Scout. 'I didn't.'

'You were the only one there,' said Scruff. 'Who else could it have been?'

Scout looked from pup to pup. They thought she was a liar and a thief, and there was nothing she could do about it. Her mum and dad would probably think so too. Scout had never felt so utterly helpless and alone.

A sharp wind ruffled Scout's fur. Dark clouds marched across the sky and big drops of rain began to fall, plip-plop-plip-plop, faster and faster. The gutters ran with water. Lightning flashed and thunder rumbled overhead. The rain poured through Scout's thick coat and dripped off the end of her nose, but the coldness she felt was deep down inside. She had been asked to leave the academy. It was all over. Her dreams were shattered. Everything had gone horribly, horribly wrong.

Scout ran out of the grounds and
into the storm. It was hard to see
through the driving rain, but Scout
ran and ran. She didn't know where
to go. She couldn't face going home,
so she ran away from the village
down to the new houses where the
river-meadows used to be.

The road was blocked. The river had finally burst its banks, and brown water was swirling into gardens and flowing through doorways. Scout could see her mum and dad helping people onto dry land.

Scout didn't want to tell her parents why she'd had to leave the academy, so she turned and ran the other way.

She ran past the hastily abandoned bungalows, which older humans liked to live in. Maybe she could hide away in one of them for a while. But the river was steadily rising and it would soon cut her off. Plastic chairs and tables were already floating in people's gardens. Despite her own misery, she was glad all the old folk had been taken to safety.

Scout stopped in her tracks. Not everyone had made it to safety!

Someone had been left behind.

A stooped figure in a long hooded raincoat was struggling out of a garden shed. Maybe he hadn't heard the rescuers. Floodwater sloshed over his boots as he headed for his bungalow.

'Hello,' woofed Scout. But the man didn't seem to hear her above the rain.

Scout watched him wade in through the front door. She knew he wouldn't be safe in his bungalow. She had to get him out of there. She had to.

She paddled through the water to the front door.

'Hello,' she woofed. 'Hello.'

A sausage floated past her through the open door. Scout stared at it as it bobbed along to join the river.

She walked in and pushed open another door to the kitchen. The old man was in the kitchen with his back to her. He was holding a sausage and reaching into the fridge for a bottle of tomato ketchup.

There was something odd about the man, she thought. It wasn't so much the way he squeezed tomato ketchup all over his sausage. It was the way a long tail was sticking out from the bottom of his raincoat.

'Frank Furter!' exclaimed Scout.

Frank spun round and glared at her, tomato ketchup all over his paws.

'I've caught you red-pawed!' said Scout. 'So this is how you've been stealing the sausages. You've been pretending to be a human!'

'Pesky pup!' said Frank, grabbing his bag of sausages. 'I'm out of here.'

'Not so fast!'

'Frank Furter, we arrest you in the name of the paw!'

Scout turned around to the voices she recognized.

'Mum! Dad!'

She watched while they put paw-cuffs on Frank.

'How did you know I was here?' said Scout.

'Major Bones came to find us to say you'd been asked to leave the academy,' said Scout's mum.

'Oh!' said Scout. She looked down at the water swirling in the kitchen.

'We saw you heading this way so we came to look for you.'

'You think I stole the Crunchie Munchies too, don't you?' said Scout.

Scout's dad put his big paw round her. 'Of course we don't,' he said. 'We know you could never do a thing like that. We came to find you because we knew you'd be upset.'

'You believe me?' said Scout.

Scout's mum smiled. 'Of course we do. We know you're loyal, brave, and true.'

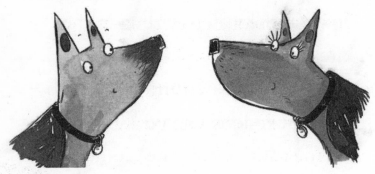

It felt as if a heavy weight had been lifted from Scout's chest.

'Thank you,' she said. 'But it still doesn't solve the mystery of the missing Crunchie Munchies.'

'No,' said her dad. 'But you've solved the mystery of the sausage thief.'

Frank glared at Scout. 'If it hadn't been for your do-gooding ways, I'd have been long gone by now.'

Scout's mum smiled. 'Thanks to you, Scout, the Little Barking Sausage Festival can go ahead again this year.'

GRRRRR...

The river had risen even higher.

'Come on,' said Scout's dad. 'We'll need to doggy-paddle out of here, and quickly!'

As Scout followed her parents and Frank through the front gate, she heard cries for help coming from the garden shed.

'HELP US, HEEEELP! HELP! OVER HERE! SAVE US!'

'Stop!' Scout shouted to her mum and dad, but they were ahead of her, carrying Frank through the water.

'HELP US, HEEEELP! HELP!'

Someone needed help.
Without thinking, Scout turned

and started swimming towards the shed. She pushed her way through the door. In the corner, Scout could see a rusty bucket swirling round and round in the dirty water. The bucket seemed to be sinking deeper and deeper.

'HELP US, HEEEELP! HELP!'

The cries were coming from inside the bucket.

A family of field mice, a mum and a dad, aunties and uncles, grandma and granddad, and lots of tiny mouselings, were clinging to the rim.

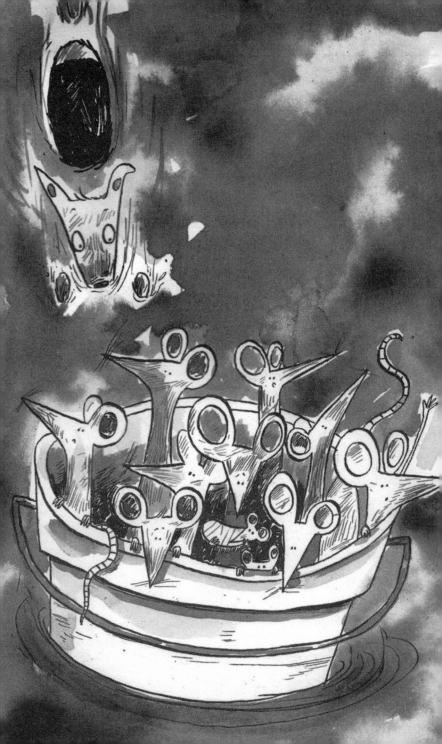

'HELP US! WATER'S COMING IN THROUGH THE HOLES!'
they called.

Scout grabbed the bucket with her teeth and pulled it from the shed. She swam and swam, dragging the mouse-filled bucket to dry ground.

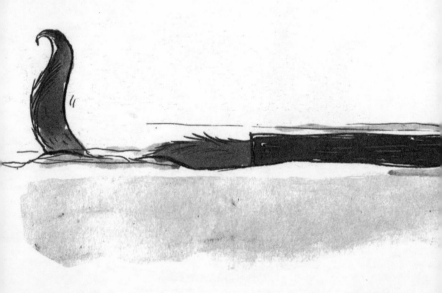

'THANK YOU FOR SAVING US,' squeaked the field mice. 'WE THOUGHT WE WERE DONE FOR.'

Scout looked in at them. Her eyes opened wide, wide, wide, because the field mice were not the only things Scout could see at the bottom of the bucket.

6

'The missing Crunchie Munchies!'
said Major Bones, picking a soggy
Crunchie Munchie from the bottom
of the bucket.

'You see, I didn't take them,'
blurted out Scout. 'The field mice
said they carried them out from the
food shed through a small crack in
the floor.'

'THIS CHANGES EVERYTHING,' said Professor Offenbach.

Scout's mum looked long and hard at Major Bones and Professor Offenbach. 'I do hope the academy remembers that everyone is innocent until proven guilty.'

'Of course, of course,' blustered Major Bones. 'Well, at least we've found the guilty culprits. It seems more than one thief has been caught today.'

The field mice clung to each other and shivered with cold.

Major Bones bent down to get a closer look at them. 'What were you thinking by stealing the pups' hard earned treats? Explain yourselves.'

RING! RING! RING! RING!

'Excuse me,' said Major Bones, 'I'd better take that call.' Major Bones looked under the blanket in his dog bed. 'Now, where did I put that phone?' he muttered.

He searched and searched until the phone rang off.

'Never mind,' said Major Bones. 'Where were we . . . ah, yes! Mice! You have been caught stealing from the academy. Scout's mum and dad will take you away and lock you up for a very, very long time.'

'Wait!' said Scout. 'You haven't listened to them. You haven't listened to their side of the story.'

'Haven't I?' said Major Bones, frowning.

'No,' said Scout. 'Shh! Let's listen.'

The mother field mouse held her tail in her paws and looked up at Major Bones. 'WE DIDN'T KNOW THE CRUNCHIE MUNCHIES WERE FOR THE PUPPIES,' she said.

'WE WERE SO HUNGRY, YOU SEE. WE USED TO LIVE ON THE

RIVER-MEADOW AND EAT THE WILD GRASSES AND FRUITS AND

SEEDS. BUT SINCE THE HUMANS BUILT THEIR HOUSES WE'VE

HAD NOWHERE TO LIVE AND NOTHING TO EAT.'

Major Bones sat down in his chair and rubbed his head. 'Oh dear,' he said. 'I see. You should have asked and we would have given you the Crunchie Munchies.'

'WE JUST WANT OUR MEADOWS BACK,' said the field mouse.

Major Bones frowned. 'Oh dear, oh dear,' he said. 'That's not so easy. What should we do?'

Scout looked around Major Bones's office, at the piles of paper

and the pens scattered on the desk
and the overflowing wastebasket.

'Why don't the mice stay here
and tidy up your office in exchange
for Crunchie Munchies, until we
can find them a new field of their
own?' said Scout.

'Well,' said Major Bones, '. . . I suppose my office could do with a bit of a tidy!'

The mice cheered squeaky cheers.
Scout looked up to see her mum
and dad beaming down at her.

'WELCOME, PUPS, AGAIN.'
Professor Offenbach had called all
the pups back into the hall.

'BEFORE WE GO HOME
TODAY, WE HAVE AN EXTRA
CELEBRATION. WE HAVE A
VERY BRAVE PUP AMONGST
US. PLEASE WELCOME SCOUT
ONTO THE GIANT SAUSAGE
PODIUM. NOT ONLY HAS

SCOUT HELPED TO CATCH A
NOTORIOUS CRIMINAL BUT,
MORE IMPORTANTLY, TODAY
SCOUT HAS SHOWN US WHAT
CARE IN THE COMMUNITY IS ALL
ABOUT. SCOUT HAS SHOWN US
THAT WE MUST TAKE TIME TO
LISTEN TO ONE ANOTHER AND
UNDERSTAND OTHERS' NEEDS
SO THAT WE CAN ALL LIVE
ALONGSIDE EACH OTHER. PLEASE
ALL WAG YOUR TAILS FOR SCOUT
FOR GAINING HER CARE IN THE
COMMUNITY BADGE.'

All the pups wagged their tails and
barked. They followed Scout to Major

Bones's office to meet the field mice and see how they were getting on.

During the ceremony, the mice had worked quickly to tidy away all the papers and put the pens and pencils neatly in the pencil pots. Major Bones's office looked like a different place.

'I'm sorry I didn't believe you, Scout,' said Gwen, hanging her head low.

'Me too,' said Lulu.

'I wouldn't lie to you,' said Scout.

'I know,' said Scruff. 'We should have trusted you. We were looking forward to the Crunchie Munchies so much and were sad to find them missing. It seemed easy to blame you.'

'Can you forgive us?' said Murphy.

'Of course,' smiled Scout. 'It's a shame we never did get any Crunchie Munchies though!'

RING! RING! RING! RING!

'Excuse me,' said Major Bones, 'I'd better take that call.'

'Here you are,' said a field mouse,
handing Major Bones the phone.
'Oh, well done!' cried Major
Bones. 'My phone! You found it!'

Major Bones held the phone to his ear. 'Yes? Major Bones here . . . really? You've been trying to get hold of me all day? I see . . . Did she? This morning, you say? Well, I never!' He glanced across at Scout several times. 'I see . . . yes, I see . . . well, that's good to know . . . thank you . . . thank you . . . I'll tell the pups the good news.'

The pups all waited to hear what Major Bones had to say.

'Well,' he said. 'That was Bernie, the head teacher's dog at the primary school. It seems that I owe Scout another apology. The reason she was late today was because she was returning a lost teddy to a child. The girl's mother is sending a big bag of Crunchie Munchies to the academy as a way of saying thank you. Scout really has earned her Care in the Community badge today.'

Scout barked. 'Crunchie Munchies all round, everyone.'

Scout trotted along with her mum
and dad to the sausage festival.

'Well,' said Dad, 'Frank is well
and truly behind bars and the Little
Barking Sausage Festival is safe for
another year.'

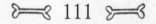

'So,' said Scout's mum, 'do you still want to be a police dog?'

'More than ever,' woofed Scout.

'Come on,' said Scout's dad, 'after all that police work, I'm hungry. Anyone want a sausage?'

Scout stared at the rows upon rows of different sausages: pork and apple, beef and onion, venison and redcurrant, bratwursts, chipolatas, chorizos, Cumberland swirls . . . so many to choose from.

'Well . . . ?' said Dad.

'I'll have a bowl of water, please,' sighed Scout. 'I think I've just about had enough of sausages until next year.'

MORE PUPPY ACADEMY STORIES COMING SOON!

GILL LEWIS
PUPPY ACADEMY
STAR
ON STORMY MOUNTAIN

GILL LEWIS
PUPPY ACADEMY
PIP
AND THE PAW OF FRIENDSHIP

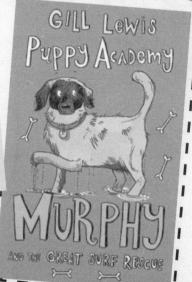

GILL LEWIS
PUPPY ACADEMY
MURPHY
AND THE GREAT SURF RESCUE

Meet Leo, A Real life police tracker DOG!

NAME
Leo

AGE
6

OCCUPATION
Police tracker dog

LIKES
Walks in the woods, tug-of-war

HATES
Bath time!

Tracked BOTH the driver and the passenger responsible for a jewel theft and found the loot as well!

Sniffer Dogs UK & International (SDUKI) is a charity closely involved with police dogs, including **Leo**!

MISSION STATEMENT
SDUKI raises money to give to any UK Police Dog Section, to replace their injured or retiring dogs.

Registration number 1141930
Find out more at www.sduki.org.uk

POLICE DOG FACTS!

The first time dogs were used by the police is believed to be 1888, when two Bloodhounds helped to track a criminal.

DID YOU KNOW?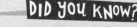

Labradors were the first police dogs used by the Metropolitan police.

German shepherds like Scout's mum and dad were first used as police dogs in London in 1948.

DID YOU KNOW?

 Police dogs normally work for about eight years.

Dogs and their handlers have to pass a test every year to make sure that they are good enough to continue working for the police.

DID YOU KNOW?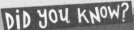

When they retire, police dogs normally go to live with their handler as a pet.

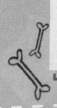

ABOUT ZAK AND HIS OWNER, GILL LEWIS

I'm **ZAK**, a German shepherd dog just like Scout. I was **GILL LEWIS**'s first dog. When she was fourteen, her wish to have a dog of her own came true and she got me. I like to think we got each other. I used to walk with her some of the way to school and meet her at the garden gate on her way home.

Some people think German shepherds are a bit fierce, but I was a big softie. I liked helping people too. I ran alongside **GiLL**'s bike when she did her paper round. I even carried some of the papers until people complained of dog slobber on their Sunday news. Like Scout, I was only trying to help . . .

Here are some other stories we think you'll love ...